QUICKREADS

TUG-OF-WAR

JANET LORIMER

SADDLEBACK
EDUCATIONAL PUBLISHING

QUICKREADS

SERIES 1

Black Widow Beauty
Danger on Ice
Empty Eyes
The Experiment
The Kula'i Street Knights
The Mystery Quilt
No Way to Run
The Ritual
The 75-Cent Son
The Very Bad Dream

SERIES 2

The Accuser
Ben Cody's Treasure
Blackout
The Eye of the Hurricane
The House on the Hill
Look to the Light
Ring of Fear
The Tiger Lily Code
Tug-of-War
The White Room

SERIES 3

The Bad Luck Play
Breaking Point
Death Grip
Fat Boy
No Exit
No Place Like Home
The Plot
Something Dreadful Down Below
Sounds of Terror
The Woman Who Loved a Ghost

SERIES 4

The Barge Ghost
Beasts
Blood and Basketball
Bus 99
The Dark Lady
Dimes to Dollars
Read My Lips
Ruby's Terrible Secret
Student Bodies
Tough Girl

SADDLEBACK
EDUCATIONAL PUBLISHING
www.sdlback.com

ISBN-13: 978-1-61651-196-8
ISBN-10: 1-61651-196-6
eBook: 978-1-60291-918-1

Printed in Guangzhou, China
0310/03-20-10

15 14 13 12 11   1 2 3 4 5

■ ■ ■

"**H**ey, I like try da kine."

With a sigh, Malia MacLeod silently counted to ten. Then she turned to face the student who was tapping her shoulder. It was Puna, the rascal, the kid who seemed to enjoy making each and every day more difficult for her.

"Puna," Malia said calmly, "ask again—in proper English this time."

The boy's grin widened. "I did say it in English. *Pidgin English!*" Puna howled with laughter.

Malia started to count to ten again, but then she gave up. She'd just have to accept that most people in Hawaii spoke the dialect.

Pidgin English was as much a part of Hawaii's culture as eating *poi* or dancing *hula.*

"Okay," Malia said with a sigh, "what do you mean by *da kine?*"

"You know," Puna said with a grin, *"the kind.* It means anything you want it to mean." Then he pointed at the new computer and said, "I like try that!" Malia nodded. As she turned to help another student, the bell rang. For a few minutes there was confusion in the classroom as students hurried out the door. When it was quiet, Malia dropped into her chair, gazing at the empty room. She loved teaching, but at the end of each day, she felt burned out.

"Of course, I'm still new here," she told herself as she straightened her desk. "It isn't unusual that the students are still testing me. I wonder if they'll ever accept me."

Then a shadow fell across the desk, and Malia looked up. Her cousin, Alani, smiled down at her. "I thought I'd drop by and see how you're doing," he said.

Malia smiled back. "You mean, to see if I'm surviving?" she asked. "I don't know, Alani. The jury is still out."

Alani chuckled. "I also came to tell you about a family party this Saturday. It's a baby *lu'au*."

Malia smiled and shook her head in bewilderment. "A *what?*"

"In the old days, most babies died before they were a year old," Alani explained. "So when a baby survived that first year, the family celebrated with a baby *lu'au*. We still celebrate the first birthday in the same way."

Malia nodded. "It sounds like fun. Who's the lucky child?"

"Your cousin Noelani's baby. You haven't met them yet, but you will." Then he told Malia what to bring. "I'll pick you up about noon," he added.

"Hold on," Malia said. "I didn't say that I could—"

"Tutu said you must come," Alani went on. "She said I'm to bring you."

Malia felt her stomach tighten. Since

she'd arrived in Hawaii two months ago, her grandmother had made many demands. Malia was beginning to resent it. But before she could say another word, Alani headed out the door. "See you on Saturday!" he called out as he disappeared down the hallway.

Malia took a deep breath and started counting to ten. "I sure seem to do a lot of counting these days," she muttered crossly. While she erased the boards, she wondered again if coming to Hawaii had been such a good idea.

■ ■ ■

Malia had been born in the Hawaiian Islands. Her mother was Hawaiian, but her father was *haole*—Caucasian. When Malia was three years old, her parents moved to the mainland. Malia had been raised in Los Angeles.

In California, she had lots of cousins on her father's side of the family. But she'd always yearned to go back to Hawaii for a long visit. She wanted to know her Hawaiian family, too. But there'd never been enough money to pay for such a trip. Still, Malia had promised herself that someday she would return to her homeland.

After graduating from college, Malia started teaching in Los Angeles. Then one day she'd learned that Hawaii was recruiting teachers from the mainland. She could hardly believe her luck. Here was her chance to live *and* work in Hawaii for a year! That would give her plenty of time to get to know her Hawaiian relatives. She could hardly wait to turn in her application.

Malia was thrilled when she was selected to teach in a rural high school on Oahu's Leeward Coast. But when she arrived, the place was much different than she'd imagined. The Leeward Coast—on the western side of the island—was much dryer than the eastern side. Malia was amused to see cactus growing on the hills.

She rented a small apartment a few blocks from the beach. The area was so beautiful! For a while Malia felt she was living in a dream.

Coconut palms and mango trees grew in her backyard. Beautiful sunsets, colorful rainbows, and amazingly bright flowers grew everywhere.

The only problem seemed to be her pushy family. Her Hawaiian relatives—especially Tutu, her grandmother—expected a lot of her. They counted on Malia to be at every family gathering. And they expected her to become active in Hawaiian political issues. Yet at the same time, Malia noticed that they seemed rather reserved around her.

Tutu had explained why. "Malia, sometimes you act so *haole*," the old woman said with a smile.

"I *am haole*," Malia replied. "Half *haole*. But what's wrong with that?"

"Nothing," the old woman said with a sad shake of her head. "Only that there's so much you need to learn about the *kanaka maoli*— the Hawaiian people. *Auwe!* I can't believe that your mother didn't teach you more about this!" The old woman looked disappointed.

Malia felt a stab of annoyance. "My

parents raised me to survive in Los Angeles," she said curtly. "I'm sorry, Grand— I mean, Tutu. I'm a California girl, no matter where I was born."

Tutu's eyes widened in shock, and Malia realized she'd hurt the old woman. She was sorry about that—but she knew she had to be firm. She didn't plan to spend the rest of her life in Hawaii. She'd signed on for just one year!

"Malia," Tutu said softly, taking her granddaughter's hand in hers. "You are *also* Hawaiian. No matter where you live, that will never change. Hawaii is more than just your birthplace. It's part of your heritage. You know about your *haole* roots, don't you?"

Malia shook her head. "Not really. Dad never thought that was important."

Tutu rolled her eyes. "Child! How can you decide where you're going if you don't know where you're from?"

Malia shrugged and looked away.

That night a familiar bad dream came back to haunt her. As a little girl, she'd had the dream many times. When Malia had asked her mother what it meant, Mama said that dreams were nonsense. They meant nothing.

In the dream, Malia always found herself in a crowd of people. They were dressed strangely, especially the women. One woman in particular seemed to stand out. Malia could tell that the people had gathered for some purpose, but she didn't understand it. When she awoke, Malia always had tears on her cheeks, although she had no idea why.

In time, the dream seemed to go away, and Malia forgot all about it. But it returned after she met her Hawaiian grandmother. Now, however, she recognized the strange costumes the women in her dream were wearing. The flowing gowns were Hawaiian *muʻumuʻu*—the long, loose dresses introduced by the haole missionaries in the early 1800s. But these were not modern *muʻumuʻu*. Somehow, Malia knew that she was dreaming about a time long before her birth.

■ ■ ■

On Saturday, Alani picked up Malia in his battered old truck. If he could tell that she was still annoyed, he didn't show it. "You're going to have a great time," he said, as he turned off the highway onto a dirt road.

Malia just grunted. Clouds of red dust swirled up from the tires as the truck bounced over the ruts. At last they pulled into a clearing. Alani parked in front of a small wooden house. Malia spotted her grandmother on the front porch. Tutu reached out and greeted her with a warm hug.

The afternoon began well enough. Alani showed Malia the *imu*—a pit in which food was cooked. Then Malia joined the other family members as Noelani opened gifts for her one-year-old. Later, sitting at one of the long picnic tables in the yard, Malia ate until she thought her stomach would burst. Everything was delicious, even the pickled *limu*—seaweed.

After the meal, Malia helped clear off the tables. For the first time since arriving in Hawaii, she felt as if she really belonged. "Maybe I should stay here longer than a year," she thought.

Then, suddenly, harsh words pierced the warm air. Several cousins were grumbling about the rights of Hawaiians to govern themselves. Alani called to Malia. "Cousin, come over here, join us. You need to hear this!"

"Here we go again," Malia thought. She shook her head. "I'm sorry, Alani, but I don't see how that concerns me."

Everyone stopped talking. They were all staring at her. "Oh, she's so *haole!*" Noelani grumbled mockingly.

That hurt. Malia spun about and walked into the house.

Tutu took one look at Malia's face and reached out her arms. Near tears, Malia went to her grandmother for comfort. "I don't belong here," she sobbed. "I never will."

"Malia, you have to understand," Tutu

said soothingly. "*Many* wrongs have been done to the Hawaiians. That's why there's a lot for you to learn."

Malia sighed. She wished she'd brought her own car so she could go home. Instead, she had to wait until Alani was ready to go. "So I'll wait," she muttered to herself, "but I won't be a part of their political talk."

She curled up in a comfortable chair in Noelani's living room. She could hear the ongoing conversation through the open windows. Several of her cousins were talking about something that would happen in January. At the same time, another cousin began to softly strum his ukulele. Bit by bit, the words and the gentle music blurred together as Malia leaned back and fell asleep.

■ ■ ■

The dream returned. Malia was in a crowd of people standing outside a huge stone building. Everyone seemed angry and upset. Malia glanced at the woman standing next to her and saw tears streaming down her cheeks.

"What's wrong?" Malia asked the woman. "Please, tell me what's wrong!"

"*Wake up!*" Malia's eyes snapped open as she heard her grandmother's voice. She blinked in confusion. Tutu was gazing at her worriedly.

Suddenly Malia realized that her cheeks were wet. She wiped away the tears, feeling embarrassed. "I—I guess I had a bad dream," she stammered. "Maybe I ate too much pickled *limu.*"

Malia hoped her lame joke would ease the tension, but Tutu frowned. "What were you dreaming about?" the old woman asked.

"It was nothing," Malia said. "I don't even remember." She struggled out of the overstuffed chair. "I really have to get home, Tutu. Is Alani ready?"

"You were talking in your sleep!" Tutu exclaimed. "You cried out, 'Hawaii for the Hawaiians'!"

Malia shrugged. "I'm telling you, I don't

remember, Tutu. I have to go now!"

Tutu's eyes narrowed a little as she studied her granddaughter. At last she nodded. Malia hugged Tutu goodbye, but she didn't dare to look her grandmother straight in the eye. She had a bad feeling that Tutu knew she wasn't telling the truth about her dream.

The next day, a strange feeling of depression settled over Malia. "This isn't like me," she thought crossly. But she couldn't shake the unhappy feeling. Finally, that afternoon, she went to talk to the school principal.

"I made a big mistake coming to Hawaii," she told him. "I'm afraid I'm going to have to break my contract."

Mr. Fernandez frowned. "Malia, that wouldn't look good on your record. Why don't you think it over for a while?" He leaned forward, looking serious. "You've been working too hard. You need to take some time off. Go sightseeing, play tourist. Have some fun." His serious look melted with a smile.

"I bet sometimes it feels like you're living in another country, doesn't it? All the strange words and foods and customs?"

Malia gasped. "How did you know?" she asked, relieved that someone finally seemed to understand.

He grinned at her. "I've had to deal with a few homesick *malihini* in my time." Seeing Malia's puzzled look, Mr. Fernandez translated. "*Malihini*—newcomers—like you."

She smiled weakly. Mr. Fernandez had put his finger on part of what was bothering her. She *was* very homesick.

The next morning Malia's mind was on the weekend ahead. She had decided to give Mr. Fernandez's suggestion a try. "TGIF," Malia thought as she opened the door to her classroom. "Thank goodness it's Friday!"

■ ■ ■

Malia was writing assignments on the board as her students filed into the classroom. Then she suddenly realized that the room seemed very quiet. She turned and saw that her students were sitting up straight at their desks. They seemed to be watching her with serious expressions. "Okay, kids, what's this about?" Malia asked.

Puna spoke first. "Mr. Fernandez, he says you like go home."

"I *want to* go home," Malia corrected. She saw that her efforts were wasted. The students were upset, but not over their grammar.

"Ms. MacLeod, no!" several students said. "You *have* to stay. We need you."

Malia gazed at them in surprise. "I thought—"

"We like the way you teach," one of the girls told Malia. "And you're nice. You try hard. You want us to learn."

Another girl raised her hand. "Have we done something wrong? Is that why you want to leave?"

Malia shook her head. She tried to explain how homesick she felt, how strange things seemed in Hawaii.

"But you're Hawaiian, aren't you?" the girl asked.

Malia nodded. "Part Hawaiian. But I'm also part *haole*. And I'm not sure the people here like that part of me."

Suddenly all the students began talking at once, telling Malia about themselves. As she tried to sort out what they were saying, she realized she had a small United Nations right there in her classroom. Chinese, Japanese, Filipino, Samoan, Scottish, Irish, Portuguese, French, Tongan, Korean, Mexican—the list went on and on!

"Please don't leave," Puna begged. "You tell us to never give up!"

Malia sighed. "Well, okay. I'll think about it," she promised.

■ ■ ■

The next morning, Malia tucked a map of Honolulu into her purse.

"Historic Honolulu, here I come!" she thought as she climbed into her car.

Two hours later, she reached the

downtown section of the capital city. She'd made a list of places she wanted to visit, beginning with 'Iolani Palace. She was anxious to see the only royal palace in the United States.

After parking a few blocks away, she walked toward the palace, feeling as if she were in a different world. The crowded streets of the bustling city were so different from the quiet little town on the Leeward Coast.

Suddenly, Malia looked up and gasped. Just ahead lay the majestic stone palace that had been built over 100 years before. But what shocked Malia was that it was the same stone building she had seen in her dream!

Malia hurried back to her car and drove straight to her grandmother's house. Tutu took one look at her face and put her ironing aside. "What's wrong, child?" she asked softly, as she led Malia to the sofa.

Then Malia told her grandmother everything, especially about the dream. "My mother said it meant nothing," she said in a shaky voice. "When you asked about it, I didn't want to admit that it was still upsetting me."

Tutu nodded. "Wait!" she said. She left the room. When she returned, she was carrying a framed picture. She silently handed it to Malia.

Malia gazed at the old photo in its dark frame. She had trouble catching her breath. "How did you know?" she whispered. "That's the woman in my dream. Tutu, I don't understand. What's this all about? Who is she?"

Tutu smiled sadly. "She was *my* tutu," the old woman said. "When she was a young woman, a terrible thing happened to our people. In those days, Hawaii was a monarchy. We were ruled by our beloved queen—Liliʻuokalani."

Tutu stood up and began to pace. Malia could see that her grandmother was very upset. "But greedy *haole* businessmen wanted Hawaii to be controlled by the United States," Tutu went on in an angry voice. "In January 1893, those men did a shameful thing. They brought in armed U.S. Marines to make the queen give up her throne. She was imprisoned in ʻIolani Palace. Then the men forced her to sign a paper giving up her throne."

Tutu's face was sad as she looked at Malia. "That was how the United States stole our kingdom," she said.

Malia shook her head in disbelief. "I never learned anything about such a thing when I was in school."

Tutu shrugged. "It's nothing for the United States to be proud of," she said bitterly. "And there's more, Malia. After that, our people were discouraged from speaking their own language. And they weren't supposed to practice their own customs and traditions anymore."

Malia felt nearly overwhelmed by waves of sadness. How could one group of people be so cruel to another? Then she thought again about her recurring dream. "Am I dreaming about the day the queen lost her throne?" she asked.

Tutu sat down again beside her granddaughter. "I think somehow you are. Do you remember the words you said in your sleep?"

Malia shook her head. Tutu repeated them. *"Hawaii for the Hawaiians* was one of the queen's slogans. Poor woman! She tried so hard to get her country back for her people."

"But how would *I* have known that?" Malia wondered aloud.

"Malia—you are named for my grandmother," Tutu went on. "Perhaps her spirit is reaching out to you, trying to tell you something."

Malia shook her head. "This is unbelievable."

"Remember, child—until you know where you've been, you can't know where you are going," Tutu said gently.

■ ■ ■

Where you have been! Malia decided the time had come to find out about her roots. Not just the history of her mother's people—but also the history of her father's family.

She was about to leave Tutu's when Alani burst through the front door. Seeing Malia, his eyes widened in surprise. "There's a rumor going around about you! I heard you want to quit teaching and go back to the mainland. Is it true?"

Malia sighed. It was hard to keep a secret in a small town. "I don't know," she groaned. "I can't make up my mind."

Then she saw the look of sadness on Tutu's face. "Oh, Malia, don't leave," Tutu said. "Promise me that you'll stay till the end of December."

Malia smiled. "Yes, that I can do, Tutu. Besides, now I have a lot of history homework to catch up on."

Over the next few weeks, Malia took every opportunity to study. Her students teased her about the tall pile of books on her desk. "You have homework, Ms. MacLeod? But you're a grownup and you're all *pau*—finished with school."

Malia laughed. "I may not be a student like you, but that doesn't mean I've quit learning. I plan to keep learning until the day I die!"

Puna whistled as he read the titles of the books. "How come you get so many books on Scotland? What does Scotland have to do with Hawaii?"

Malia explained about her Scottish ancestors. "It's time I learned where I came from," she said.

Her interest sparked her students' curiosity about their own backgrounds. Now all of them wanted to know where their ancestors had come from.

Mr. Fernandez stopped Malia on the walkway one afternoon. "Do you still plan to go back home?" he asked.

Malia shrugged. "I haven't made up my mind," she said. "For sure, I'll be here until the end of December. After that . . ." Her voice trailed away.

The principal shook his head. "You're

such a good teacher, Malia. Take this family-tree project of yours. The students love it! Even that rascal Puna is visiting the school library on a regular basis these days. It would be a real shame if we lost you."

With a heavy heart, Malia watched him walk away. She didn't want to disappoint him or her students. But she didn't want to disappoint herself, either.

On a Saturday afternoon in late November, Malia was curled up with one of her history books when the phone rang. It was Alani. "Why aren't you at the beach?" he demanded.

Malia laughed. "Because I'm busy reading."

"Tutu's been asking about you," Alani said. "Everyone here misses you."

Suddenly Malia realized that she missed her cousins, too. "What, no more *lu'au?*" she teased.

Alani laughed. "You're beginning to sound like a local," he said. "As a matter of fact, there's a family get-together coming up next week. We want to talk about how to mark the anniversary of the overthrow in January."

"The overthrow of the monarchy?" Malia asked. "Do you mean when the queen lost her throne?"

"Yeah," Alani said in surprise. "Good work, cousin! You're learning."

Malia had the word "no" on the tip of her tongue. But at the last moment she changed her mind. "As a matter of fact," Malia said slowly, "I'd *love* to come. Just tell me when and where."

"This is great," Alani cried out. "I didn't think you'd want to."

"Why not?" Malia asked.

"Because—well, you know!"

"Because I'm so *haole?*" Malia asked. She could almost hear Alani squirming.

"Yeah, something like that, I guess," he laughed in embarrassment.

Malia laughed, too. "It's been a while now since I arrived in Hawaii," she said. "I've learned a lot. And I'd like to share something with the family. Believe me, I have a story to tell!"

■ ■ ■

Malia sat on a rock and gazed out at the ocean. Today, the water was a beautiful blue-green. Foamy white waves crashed on the shore. Behind her, Malia heard her cousins talking and laughing as they prepared the food. She took a deep breath. The fresh salt air of the ocean was mixed with the delicious aroma of barbecued meat.

Then someone tapped her shoulder. "Are you ready to tell your story?" Alani asked. Malia nodded. "I told everyone how hard you've been working," he went on. "We're all proud of you, Malia. It's really wonderful that you're finally learning about your heritage."

Malia gazed at Alani. He looked pleased with himself and a little smug. She smiled as she thought to herself, "Boy oh boy, have I got a surprise for you, cousin."

When everyone had gathered around, Malia began to speak. "Long, long ago," she said, "a large country overpowered a smaller, weaker one. The people in the weak country lost their ruler. They were ordered not to speak their own language or wear any of their native costumes. They weren't allowed to play their own instruments or dance their native dances."

Malia saw that her listeners were paying close attention.

"They were forbidden to practice their customs and traditions," Malia went on. "Today, the descendants of these people are trying to gain more power over their country and their own lives."

"You've learned well," Alani said. "Hawaii's story is indeed a sad one. And I'm proud of you for—"

"Oh, no—I wasn't talking about Hawaii," Malia cut in. Her cousin blinked in surprise. "Huh?" he said.

"I'm talking about Scotland," Malia went on. "In 1746, the Highland clans fought the English at a place in Scotland called Culloden Field. The Scots lost the battle. After that, the English did everything they could to wipe out their enemy completely."

"What does that have to do with Hawaii?" Alani asked. He sounded annoyed—as if Malia's story had wasted everyone's time.

"I'm getting there," Malia said with a smile. "After the Battle of Culloden, many Scots moved to other countries to start new lives. Some of them settled in Hawaii. In fact, there may have been some Scots who were involved in the overthrow of the monarchy."

Malia saw the frowns on her cousins' bewildered faces.

"When I learned that," Malia said, "I felt like I was caught in a game of tug-of-war. Remember that I'm half Scottish, half Hawaiian. I didn't know whether to be proud of my heritage or ashamed."

Alani shook his head in irritation. "But you live in Hawaii!" he exclaimed. "Don't you see? It's *Hawaiian* history you have to think about."

"Hawaiian history, Scottish history! It doesn't matter—the story is the same. There's nothing I can do about the past, Alani," Malia explained. "I can't go back and change history. I can't right the old wrongs. *None of us can."*

"But if enough Hawaiians protest what was done—" Noelani started to say.

Malia interrupted her cousin's words. "What I *can* do is try my best to see that the same mistakes aren't made today. I can work to keep history from repeating itself. Not here, not anywhere."

"How do you plan to do that?" asked Tutu.

Malia grinned. "Well, for starters, by staying here in Hawaii. This place is beginning to grow on me. Next, by being the best possible teacher I can. I want to encourage my students to go on learning about themselves and each other. And last but not least, by teaching them to respect each other and stop making fun of each other's differences."

"Oh, Malia, that's *wonderful!"* Tutu cried out, reaching out to hug her granddaughter.

"Do you know one of the most important things I've learned? It's that Hawaii is like a mixed salad," Malia finished. "Each fruit or vegetable tastes delicious all by itself. But when they're all mixed together, they taste even better. That's what makes Hawaii so special."

Tutu laughed. "A good way to put it, granddaughter. Now let's eat."

After-Reading Wrap-Up

1. Why is *Tug-of-War* a fitting title for the story?

2. What incident sparked Malia's interest in her heritage?

3. What are the similarities between the British overthrow of the Scots and the U.S. government's overthrow of the Hawaiian rulers?

4. Why did Malia compare her classroom to the United Nations?

5. What did Malia plan to do to "keep history from repeating itself"?

6. What happened at the battle of Culloden?